Hugs & Kisses, God

from Kids Around the World

By Allia Zobel Nolan

Illustrated by Miki Sakamoto

*"For God, my husband, Des, and kids around
the world ... hugs & kisses."* AZN

ZONDERVAN.com/
AUTHORTRACKER
follow your favorite authors

We're all children of this great big world—from Maine to Timbuktu.

When I wake up
in the morning,
I get on my knees
and pray.

4

I send hugs and kisses to the Lord.

That's how I start my day.

My nose leads me to my breakfast—yummy pancakes on my plate.
I write "Love You, God," with syrup.
Then I tell him, "God, you're great!"

5

6

Daddy walks me to my day school.
On the way, we get a thrill.

"Hugs and kisses,
God," I whisper,

"for those daisies
on the hill."

Being nice to other people—that is how we show God love.
We know he'll be happy when he looks down from above.

I invite God to a party.
Tie balloons on everything.

Then I tell him,
"God, I love you.

I'm your princess;
you're my King!"

Gran and I—we read the Bible. That's the way we give God glory.
I learn all about what God has done from every Bible story.

Sometimes when I blow bubbles,
God gives me a big surprise.

I say, "Love You, God,"
and "Thanks,"

for rainbows right
before my eyes.

I show God how much I love him by behaving for my mother.
He must surely know I care because I share things with my brother.

On the days that I feel lonely,
I take walks and tell God news.

Then I send him love and kisses,
and that chases all my blues.

Every day God sends us blessings, filled with love we can't ignore.
So we send him hugs and kisses ... then we send him zillions more.

We love summer and the time we get to play beneath pink skies.

We send "hugs and kisses" to the Lord for flashing fireflies.

When it's night, if we could gather stars that twinkle way up high,